She didn't even wake up
to chase and catch the other animals.
They simply just tripped over her.

One day Cheetah heard a **crash!** of thunder and a **flash!** of lightning, and the sound of the little Vervet Monkeys calling,

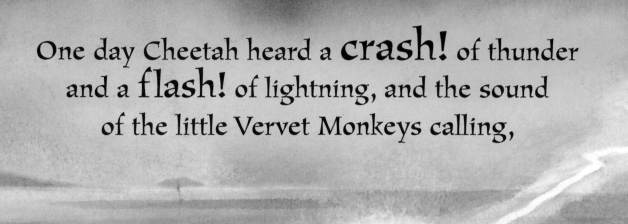

"Wake up, Sleepy Cheetah!
Wake up!"

SLeePY CheeTah

Written by
Mwenye Hadithi

Illustrated by
Adrienne Kennaway

Hodder
Children's
Books

Long ago, on the sandy African Plain, Cheetah liked to snooze in the sun. In those days she was the colour of hot sand, so she was very hard to see.

Sleepy Cheetah opened one eye but she was too sleepy to get up and see what the matter was.

The other animals were running across the sandy plain towards the rushing river.

The little Vervet Monkeys scampered towards Cheetah across a patch of burnt grass.

"Wake up, Sleepy Cheetah!" they called.
"We can see Fire! Wake up and run!"

The little Vervet Monkeys bounced on Cheetah's sandy back with their black sooty paws.

"Wake up, Sleepy Cheetah! Wake up and run!"

"Run?" muttered Sleepy Cheetah. "I can't run. My paws are too soft."

So the little Vervet Monkeys bounced on Cheetah's sandy tummy.

"Wake up, Sleepy Cheetah! Wake up and run!"

"Run?" muttered Sleepy Cheetah. "I can't run. My legs are too short."

The biggest Vervet Monkey bounced all over
Cheetah's sandy tail. He even bounced on her
head. "Wake up, Sleepy Cheetah!"
he called. "You can run if you try!"

Sleepy Cheetah just rolled over
and went back to sleep.

"Run!" called Elephant as he hurried past.

"Run!" called the Impalas
as they rushed past.

"Run!" called Rhino as she charged past.

"Run!" called the Giraffes as they galloped past.

Suddenly Cheetah felt her tail getting hot.

She stood up and started to walk.

Then she started to trot.

Then she started to run.

Soon she found herself racing like the wind
across the sandy African Plain away from the fire.

"Run faster!" called Cheetah, running like the whistling wind past the Impalas.

"Run faster!" called Cheetah,
running like the lightning past Elephant.

"Run faster!" called Cheetah, running like the rushing river past the Giraffes.

"Run faster!" called Cheetah, running
like the rolling clouds past Rhino.

She ran so fast the wind made her eyes water
as if she was crying. But she didn't stop.

"Jump on my back!" she called
    to the little Vervet Monkeys when
        they finally came to the river.

With a **flying leap,** she jumped over the water and landed on the other side.

When the animals were safely across the river, they watched the fire fade and disappear as it reached the water.

"Thank you, Cheetah," said the little Vervet Monkeys as they climbed down from her back.
"That was fun! Can we jump across the river again?"

The animals turned to look at Cheetah
and began to laugh.

"Look!" said the little Vervet Monkeys.
"You're covered in our sooty paw prints. And
the wind has left sooty streaks on your face!"

"What a beautiful coat you have now,"
said Leopard. "Like mine but more sandy."

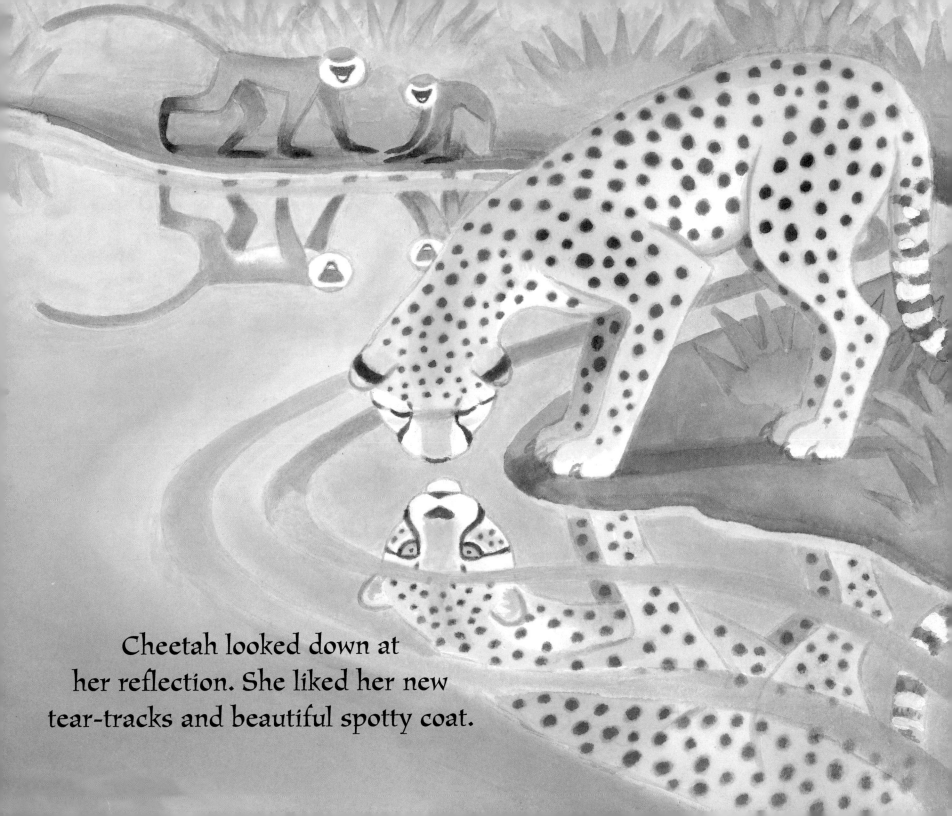

Cheetah looked down at her reflection. She liked her new tear-tracks and beautiful spotty coat.

And to this day, Cheetah is the fastest runner of all
the animals, faster than Lion, and as fast as the
wind racing across the sandy African Plain.